Disney's
# My Very First Winnie the Pooh™

# The Very Best
# Berry Pie

Written by
## Tammi J. Santa Croce

Illustrated by
## Atelier Philippe Harchy

SCHOLASTIC INC.
New York Toronto London Auckland Sydney
Mexico City New Delhi Hong Kong Buenos Aires

*For Pépé and for John—TSC*

Published by Scholastic Inc., 90 Old Sherman Turnpike, Danbury, CT  06816
by arrangement with Disney Licensed Publishing.

SCHOLASTIC and associated logos are trademarks
and/or registered trademarks of Scholastic Inc.

ISBN 0-7172-6565-X

Printed in the U.S.A.

One morning, Pooh woke up and rubbed his eyes. Sunlight streamed in through the window.

"Today is a perfect day to go fishing!" he said happily. "I'll ask Piglet to go with me." Pooh got out of bed, and as he was stretching, he heard a knock at his door.

"Pooh! Are you awake?" a small voice said. It was Piglet!

"Come in, Piglet!" Pooh cried, opening the door. "I was just thinking of you. Isn't it a wonderful day? Let's go fishing at the pond!"

"I'd love to, Pooh," Piglet replied. "B-but I've been thinking about something else I'd like to do first. Kanga is always doing such nice things for us—taking us on picnics, inviting us over for tea. W-wouldn't it be nice to do something special for her?"

Pooh smiled a big smile and thought about his friend Kanga. *No matter how busy she is, she always finds time to offer me a smackerel of honey*, he thought. "Piglet, that's a grand idea. But what should we do?"

"Well," Piglet said, "how about making a special surprise pie just for Kanga? We could ask all our friends to help collect berries."

"Splendid!" Pooh said. "We can keep the berries that we collect in my nightcap." Pooh looked around the room. "Oh, bother," he said. "Where did it go? Piglet, will you help me find my nightcap?"

Pooh and Piglet searched Pooh's house— behind the chair, under the bed, in the cupboard full of empty honey pots. Finally, Piglet spotted the nightcap behind Pooh's bed, and the two friends set out to find their pals.

$\mathcal{M}$eanwhile, Tigger and Roo were playing a game of hide-and-seek in the woods.

"I'll count, li'l buddy, and you hide," Tigger said to Roo. Tigger turned toward the tree and covered his eyes. He began to count. "1...2...3..."

*I've got the best hiding place!* Roo thought excitedly as he ducked into a big log and waited for Tigger to finish counting. Roo could hardly keep from giggling.

"…18…19…20. Ready or not, here I come!"
Tigger yelled. He looked in a bush, up a tree,
behind a rock—but he couldn't find Roo.

"Hmmm," Tigger said, scratching his head. "That little guy sure knows how to hide!"

After a few more minutes of searching for Roo, Tigger began to worry.

"OK!" Tigger shouted. "I give up! Where are you?"

"Here I am!" Roo squeaked as he crawled out of the log. He bounced over to Tigger.

Tigger smiled. "Roo, li'l buddy, you're the bestest hider there is!"

"Let's play over here now!" Roo said and hopped farther down the path.

Just then, Tigger and Roo saw Pooh and Piglet coming their way. Roo scrambled back to where Tigger was.

"Pooh!" Tigger called. "And Piglet!"

"Halloo, Tigger and Roo," Pooh said. "We want to do something special for Kanga because she always does 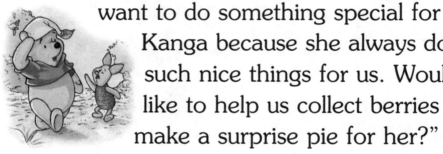 such nice things for us. Would you like to help us collect berries to make a surprise pie for her?"

Tigger bounced on his tail. "Hoo-hoo-hoo! You betcha! Tiggers love to collect berries for Mrs. Kanga!" He leaned down and whispered to Roo, "And they love eating pie even more!"

Roo giggled.

"Tigger," Piglet began, "would you and Roo go round up the rest of our friends in the Hundred-Acre Wood? Pooh and I will start looking for berries right here."

"That we will!" Tigger cried happily. And he and Roo bounced off to find the rest of the gang.

After Tigger and Roo had gone, Pooh and Piglet looked around and wondered where to start.

"Let's try over there, Pooh," Piglet suggested, pointing to a group of small bushes. Pooh searched the top of the bushes, while Piglet looked underneath.

Soon they heard some familiar voices. Tigger and Roo returned with Rabbit, Eeyore, and Christopher Robin.

"I remember the last time that Kanga invited us all over for supper," said Christopher Robin. "She made such wonderful food!"

"She even had a special plate of thistles just for me," Eeyore said.

"I say," Rabbit began, "what a splendid idea! Kanga is such a dear friend, and she deserves a wonderful surprise just like this." He wandered over to a grassy area with Christopher Robin and Tigger and started looking for berries.

The friends searched for a few minutes but turned up nothing. "Maybe we're looking in the wrong place," Christopher Robin said. "Why don't we split up and each look somewhere else?"

So Rabbit searched in the sandy pit where Roo always played. Tigger stood on a nearby cliff and looked around, then checked in some bushes. Christopher Robin and Eeyore found another patch of bushes and looked there. Pooh and Piglet looked behind some trees.

"There must be berries around here s-somewhere!" Piglet exclaimed.

"Leave it to me, Piglet!" Tigger cried. "Tiggers are tigger-ific at finding berries!" But even Tigger wasn't having any luck—although he did find lots of rocks, dirt, and insects.

Pooh thought and thought. Then he said, "Since I'm a bear of very little brain, let's ask Owl where to find the best berries."

"What a great idea, Pooh!" said Piglet. "Let's go ask Owl right now."

So Pooh and Piglet set out to find Owl. When they reached Owl's perch, Pooh said, "Owl, we want to show Kanga how much we appreciate all the nice things that she does for us. So we'd like to have a party for her and surprise her with a special berry pie. Do you know where to find the very best berries in the Hundred-Acre Wood?"

"Ah, yes!" Owl exclaimed. "I know the very place! In fact, I was there just the other day, gathering berries for myself. Come with me, my friends."

Owl flew ahead of Pooh and Piglet, who followed the path until they came to a place in the woods that was full of berry bushes!

"I will help you gather berries for a while," Owl said. "Then I must return to my housework. But I most certainly will join you at Kanga's later for the big celebration!" He picked a few berries and dropped them into Pooh's nightcap.

"Pooh, look at all these berries!" Piglet cried. "Oh, Owl, this is w-wonderful!"

"Yes," Pooh replied. "With these berries, we certainly will have the very best berry pie."

$A$s Pooh, Piglet, and Owl were busy filling Pooh's nightcap with berries, Rabbit, Eeyore, Tigger, Roo, and Christopher Robin came walking down the path. When they saw all of the berry bushes, they couldn't believe their eyes!

"Oh, my!" Rabbit exclaimed. "Look at all the berries!"

"I think there are enough berries here for at least a hundred pies," Pooh said excitedly to Rabbit.

Christopher Robin shook his head and laughed. "Silly old bear," he said. "We only need enough for one very special pie."

Everyone helped gather berries and put them into Pooh's nightcap, which was getting fuller by the minute!

Tigger decided to take a break from the berry picking. He put a few more berries in Pooh's nightcap and looked for a good spot to rest—and that's when he noticed that Roo was missing.

"Hey, everybody, where's our little buddy, Roo?" he asked. Everyone had been so busy picking berries that no one noticed Roo was gone.

"He can't be far," Rabbit said.

"We'll find him," said Christopher Robin. The friends started down the path to look for Roo.

"Roo!" Tigger called. "Where are ya?"

They passed a large log on the ground. Christopher Robin thought he heard a noise coming from the log. He knelt down and peered inside. There was Roo!

"Here he is," Christopher Robin called. "He's safe and sound asleep."

Roo opened his eyes and stretched.

Tigger peeked his head into the log. "Hey, buddy boy! Whatcha doin'? Did you think we were playing hide-and-seek again?"

Roo blinked and looked at his friends. "Picking all those berries made me tired!" he said.

"I'm with ya there, ol' buddy," said Tigger. "I was gettin' ready for a nap myself!"

"Well, I'm sure glad *that's* over!" Rabbit said with a laugh. Pooh smiled.

"Now that we know Roo is okay," said Christopher Robin, "I'll take the berries home and make the pie. When it's ready, we can all go over to Kanga's together and surprise her." Everyone said good-bye to Christopher Robin, who picked up the berries and headed home down the path.

The rest of the friends talked about what they would do until it was time for the party.

"I think I'll tend to my garden," Rabbit said.

Roo bounced up and down next to Tigger. "Let's play another game of hide-and-seek!" he said.

Pooh smiled at Piglet. "And we can go fishing at the pond now!"

"And swimming!" Piglet added.

"Splendid," Pooh said. "See you all later."

The friends waved good-bye to one another and set off down the path. Pooh went home and got his fishing pole, tackle box, and his lucky fishing hat. When he was ready, he and Piglet went to the pond.

They found a shady spot by the water and sat down.

"I'll keep you company while you fish," Piglet told Pooh.

"I'll watch you while you swim," Pooh told Piglet.

The two friends spent the rest of the afternoon taking turns fishing and swimming. Then they went back to Pooh's house to wait for the party.

"D-do you think Kanga will be surprised?" Piglet asked.

"Oh, yes, Piglet," Pooh replied. "This is going to be a wonderful party."

Just then, they heard a knock at the door. Everyone was there, including Christopher Robin, who was carrying the most scrumptious-looking pie! So they all set off for Kanga and Roo's house.

When they arrived, Pooh knocked on the door. Kanga opened it, and everyone shouted, "Surprise!"

"Oh, my!" said Kanga. "How wonderful to see all of you! Have I forgotten someone's special day?"

"No," Piglet said. "W-we just wanted to show you how much we appreciate everything you do for us."

Kanga smiled at her dear friends. "What a nice surprise," she said. "Please, come in, and let's have some of that delicious-looking pie."

Everyone gathered around the table, and Kanga set out plates. In between bites of pie, Tigger said, "This really *is* the very best berry pie!"

Kanga smiled. "It certainly is, Tigger dear," she said. "And the best part of all is sharing it with such wonderful friends."